By ... Pearson
& Steve Beckett

TITLES IN THE STRANGE TOWN SET

BIGFOOT RESCUE
THE SPACE KITTEN
SHOPPING SPREE
THOR NEXT DOOR
THE IRON STONES
EXTRA TIME
RUBBISH INVASION
GOING UNDERGROUND

Badger Publishing Limited
Oldmedow Road,
Hardwick Industrial Estate,
King's Lynn PE30 4JJ

Telephone: 01438 791037
www.badgerlearning.co.uk

2 4 6 8 10 9 7 5 3

Thor Next Door
ISBN 978-1-78464-687-5

Text © Danny Pearson 2017
Complete work © Badger Publishing Limited 2017

Publisher: Susan Ross
Senior Editor: Danny Pearson
Series Consultant: Tim Collins
Illustration: Steve Beckett
Designer: Fiona Grant

THOR NEXT DOOR

CONTENTS

Logan is not exactly happy about having to move to a town in the middle of nowhere. It looks funny, it smells funny and it even feels funny, if that's possible?

Everyone, and everything, in this town just doesn't seem right, but no one seems to care or even notice. Everyone, that is, apart from Eva. She has spent years collecting evidence of the weird goings-on in Strange Town.

Eva, Logan and his dog, Otis, are the Strange Town Squad – always ready and on the lookout for all things odd.

You are about to find out that some towns can be stranger than others.

Welcome to Strange Town.

CAST OF CHARACTERS

Logan

Eva

Otis

Dave

VOCABULARY

ancient   mighty
calories   rummaged
heroic   scoffing

Chapter One

Dave

Eva was listening to The Iron Stones' new album with Logan in her treehouse.

It had been a perfect afternoon of stuffing their faces with pizza and chilling out to music.

"Can we change the music?" asked Logan. "I want to listen to Kanye East's new album."

"Sure," replied Eva. "But you have to get up and change the music. I am stuffed."

Logan pulled himself up from the sofa and waddled over to the laptop. He looked out of the window.

"Wow! Your neighbour is scoffing even more than us."

"His name is Dave." Eva said as she rolled off the sofa. "Nice guy but he eats like a pig."

Dave was doing slow-motion laps of his driveway. He had a large chicken leg in one hand and a giant-sized coke in the other.

"Hey Dave!" shouted Eva. "How's it going?"

"Hi Eva!" Dave shouted back. "I'm good, thanks. Just walking off a few calories before dinner."

"*Before* dinner? Looks like he has started already," Logan whispered to Eva.

Eva looked into Dave's garage. She could see a large, ancient-looking hammer next to a set of weights, which were covered in cobwebs.

"Hey, Dave, what is with that cool hammer?" Eva asked.

Dave span round and ran as fast as he could up to the garage and pulled the door shut. "It's nothing. Pretend you never saw it," he said, sweating.

Dave hurried back inside his house and slammed the door shut.

SLAM!

"That was weird," said Eva as she raised one eyebrow. "I wonder why he got so spooked when I asked him about that hammer. I know I have seen it somewhere before. I'm going to go for a closer look."

"That is the silliest thing you have ever said," replied Logan shaking his head. But it was too late. Eva was running over to next-door's garage.

Chapter Two

Hammer Time

"This feels wrong," Logan said nervously. "We shouldn'
be going into someone else's garage."

"Chill out. We are only going to open it and have a
look at that hammer," Eva said as she pushed the
garage door.

They peered in and saw a stack of dusty old weights
and gym equipment. In the middle of all this clutter
was the hammer.

Eva stared at it. "I knew I'd seen this before," she
whispered. "It's Thor's hammer."

"Thor? The guy from the comic books?" asked Logan.

"Yes. No. Well, sort of," said Eva. "Thor was an Ancient Norse god. He was the god of thunder and lightning. He had a hammer that only he could use. It helped him to defeat his enemies."

"I see," said Logan. "So what is it doing in Dave's garage?"

A large shadow fell over them from behind.

"What did I tell you kids?" Dave boomed.

Eva, Logan and Otis slowly backed up into the garage as Dave stomped towards them.

He looked very angry. "I told you to pretend you never saw this, but you had to come over and spy on me anyway."

Eva could see an old wood-carving on the wall. The man in it looked like Dave. Only more heroic. He was dressed like a Viking and carrying the hammer.

"That's you, isn't it?" she asked. "You're Thor. Well, at least, you used to be."

Logan couldn't believe what she was saying. "Eva, will you shut up? You are going to make it worse. He couldn't possibly be that guy from the carving."

Dave stopped. "Oh, he is right," he said in an uneven voice. "I could never be him again. I mean, *look* at me." He stuck out his belly and began to cry.

He sank to the floor, pulled out a squashed cheeseburger that was in his back pocket and ate it with tears streaming from his eyes.

"It's not my fault. I came to Earth for a holiday over a hundred years ago and now I am stuck here. I loved it at first but then I started to eat too much. The food here... it's so good!"

"Why are you stuck here?" asked Eva.

"I got too lazy and too fat. I am no longer worthy to pick up my hammer. The hammer is the only thing that can open the gate back to my world," he sobbed.

Logan kneeled down next to him. "So all you have to do is get fit, do something heroic and become worthy again. Then you can lift the hammer and get back home?"

"Ha! Easy for you to say. I am so out of shape," said Dave as he lifted a chocolate bar from his pocket. "I'll never be worthy enough to lift my mighty hammer."

"Nonsense!" shouted Eva, slapping the chocolate bar from his hand. "We can help you become the mighty Thor again."

"Really?" asked Dave.

"Really?" asked Logan.

"Yes, really!" said Eva.

Chapter Three

Training

"Knees up! Move it, move it, *move* it!" Eva shouted as she jogged in front of Dave.

"I can't," Dave cried. "It's too hot!"

Eva turned to look at him. "Stop whining. Drop down and give me twenty."

Dave collapsed to the floor and rummaged around in his pocket. He pulled out a twenty-pound note. "Please, take it. Anything to stop this madness."

"Not twenty pounds. I mean twenty push-ups. Now!" she yelled.

Otis and Logan were looking on from the comfort of the treehouse. "Wow, Eva!" shouted Logan. "You are quite the personal trainer."

"Why, thank you," Eva said smiling. "Any luck finding something heroic for this old Viking god to do?"

Logan gazed at the local paper. "Not much I am afraid. A family have reported their kitten lost. We could start there?"

Eva shrugged her shoulders. "It's hardly the stuff of legend, but it's a start I guess." She prodded the huge figure on the ground. "Get up. It's time for you to become a hero again."

2 WEEKS LATER...

They were all back in Dave's garage. He'd been trying to lift the hammer for half an hour, but it still would not budge.

"It's no good," Logan said. "We have rescued five cats from trees, helped more than twenty old people across the road and even saved someone from being pooed on by a low-flying pigeon. Dave is never going to find anything heroic enough to do."

"We need to find something bigger," said Eva. "Only a truly heroic act will make him worthy again. What did you use to do when you were ... Thor?"

"Oh, you know," said Dave, "fighting armies, battling dragons, toppling giants, the usual sort of stuff."

"That's great," Logan sighed. "Where are we going to find a dragon round here?"

"I've got it," said Eva.

"What, a dragon?" asked Logan.

"No," said Eva. "But I may be able to find a giant."

She pulled a piece of paper from her back pocket and showed it to Logan and Dave. It showed lots of strong men and women with the words 'Wrestle Fest'.

"Felix 'the Giant' is wrestling tonight," she said. "Dave will be a hero for sure if he beats him."

"Sounds like a plan," said Logan. He held his hand up and Eva gave him a high five.

"It's alright for you," sighed Dave. "All you have to do is watch. I have to beat Felix the Giant."

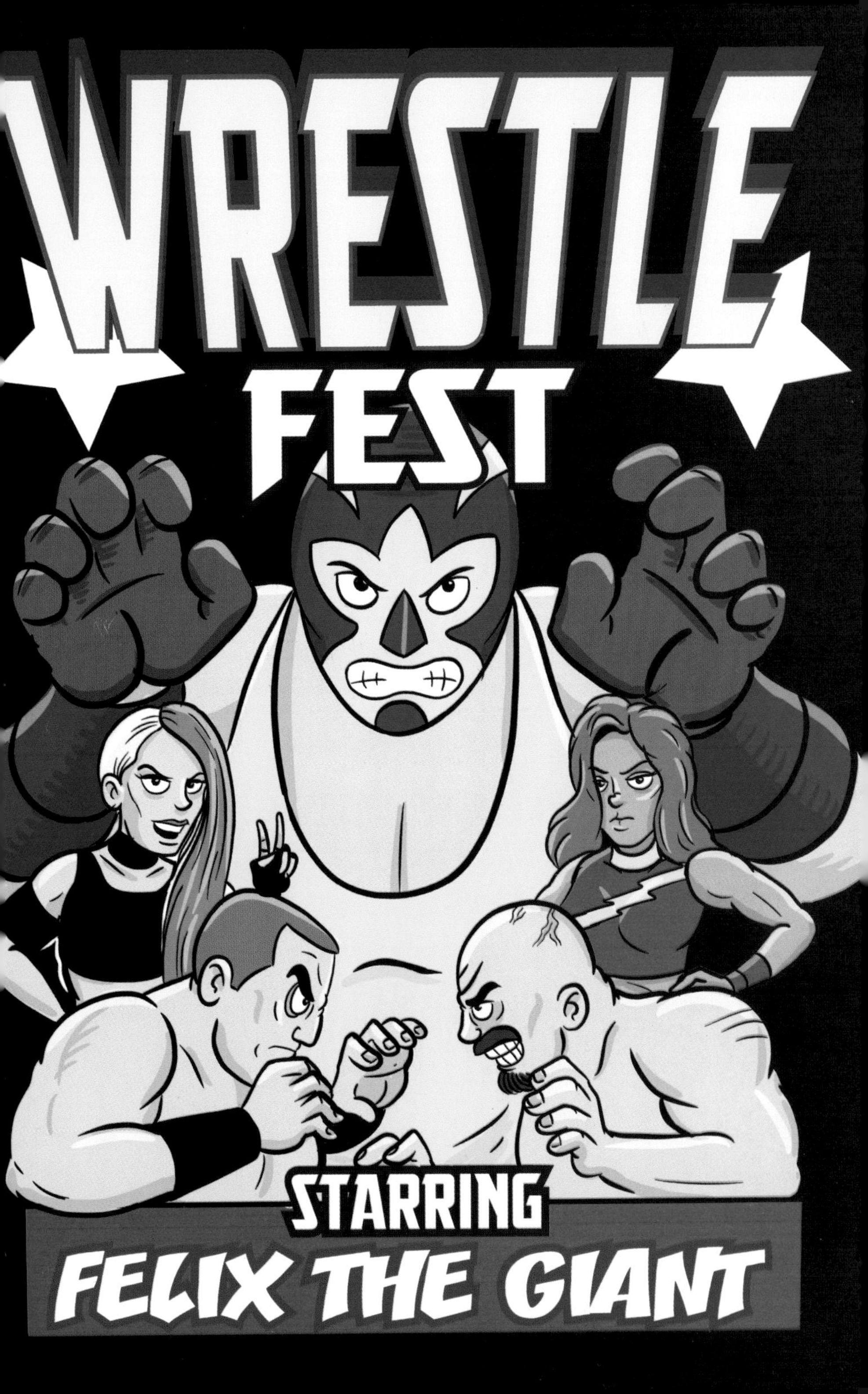
WRESTLE
FEST
STARRING
FELIX THE GIANT

Chapter Four

Stormy

Felix the Giant had just won his fourth match in a row.

"Wow! He is one mean guy," said Eva.

"One tough guy too," replied Logan.

Dave looked at the Giant. "I used to eat guys like this for breakfast. But now I eat doughnuts and chips for breakfast instead. I'll never beat him."

"You are Thor, the thunder god," said Eva. "You have nothing to fear from any puny human. Now get up there and be the hero you used to be."

The announcer stepped to the front of the ring. "Ladies and gentlemen, is there anyone else out there who dares to challenge the Giant?"

"I do," whispered Dave from the side of the ring.

The announcer bent down. "Sorry sir, did you say something?"

"I will challenge him," Dave said a little louder.

The announcer looked him up and down. "OK buddy. If you are sure. Hop on in."

The crowd cheered as Dave stepped into the ring.

The Giant looked over from his corner and let out a loud, deep laugh.

HA! HA! HA!

"You know this is a wrestling contest and not an eating one, right?" he asked.

He strode over to Dave and patted his belly. "I think climbing into the ring made you a little hungry. Would you like a sweet, tubby?"

The crowd booed as the Giant reached out of the ring and snatched a lollipop from a small girl.

"Here we go, tubby," he laughed. "Now why don't you come and get your sweetie?"

Dave started to turn red as he stomped over to the Giant. The doors of the arena blew open and a strong wind blew in.

"Stop calling me tubby and give that girl her lollipop back!" he roared.

Logan looked at Eva. "He is getting angry! The inner Thor is coming out!"

The Giant flicked Dave on the nose. "Come on tubby, let's see what you've got."

There was a violent crack of lightning and a huge rumble of thunder.

The roof of the hall tore off.

CRASHHHH!!!

Dave looked up at the sky and then back down at the Giant. "My name is not tubby. My name is THOR!"

He picked the Giant up with one hand and span him around.

"Arghh! Put me down!" the Giant roared.

"You want me to let go?" laughed Dave. "OK then."

He threw the Giant into the air and stepped aside.

The Giant rose a few feet, then plummeted down and smashed through the wrestling ring to the floor beneath, knocking him out cold.

The crowd went wild. The Giant had been defeated.

Dave picked up the lollipop and handed it back to the child. The crowd cheered and started to chant: Thor! Thor! Thor!

"You did it!" cried Logan.

"You are a hero!" shouted Eva.

Thor raised his hand to the sky. His hammer came whistling through the open roof and landed perfectly in the palm of his left hand.

He turned to Logan and Eva. "Thank you guys. If you ever have a *giant* problem again, you know who to call."

He span round and blew kisses to the crowd, then pointed his hammer up to the stormy sky. With one loud

WHOOOOOSH!

and a flash of lightning, he shot up into the air.

Logan raised his hands. "WOW! What a match, what an exit!"

"Yes! You could say that the atmosphere is electric," Eva said laughing.

QUESTIONS

1. What were Eva, Logan and Otis listening to in her treehouse? *(page 6)*

2. What could Eva see in her neighbour's garage? *(page 8)*

3. What was Dave's real name? *(page 12)*

4. What did Felix 'the Giant' steal from a small girl? *(page 23)*

5. What did the crowd chant once Dave won his match? *(page 28)*

6. What would you do if you bumped into Thor?

MEET THE
AUTHOR AND ILLUSTRATOR

THE AUTHOR

Danny Pearson landed on planet Earth during the 1980s. He assures us that the Strange Town series is based on actual events that have happened in the strange town that he lives in.

THE ILLUSTRATOR

Steve Beckett has a robot arm that is programmed to draw funny pictures. He likes playing with toy soldiers and dreams of being an ace survival expert. He is scared of heights, creepy crawlies and doesn't like camping!